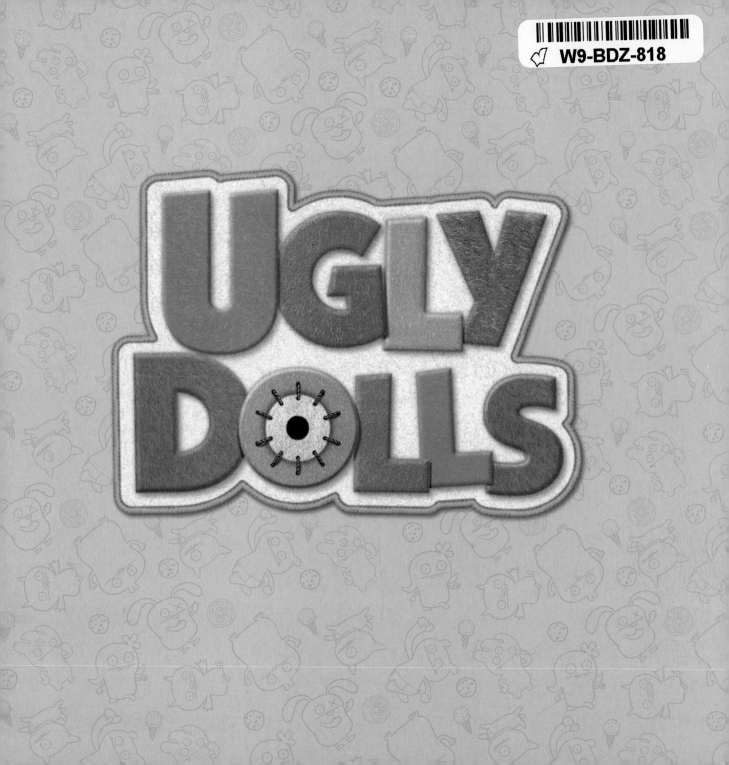

Little, Brown and Company
Hachette Book Group
1290 Avenue of the Americas, New York, NY 10104
Visit us at LBYR.com
www.uglydolls.com

First Edition: April 2019

LB kids is an imprint of Little, Brown and Company.
The LB kids name and logo are trademarks of Hachette Book Group, Inc.

The publisher is not responsible for websites
(or their content) that are not owned by the publisher.

"Couldn't Be Better" Written by Glenn Slater and Christopher Lennertz, copyright © 2018 All rights reserved. Used by permission. Reprinted by permission of STXtreme Music and STXciting Music.

ISBNs: 978-0-316-42449-3 (pbk.), 978-0-316-42452-3 (ebook), 978-0-316-42447-9 (ebook), 978-0-316-42451-6 (ebook)

Printed in the United States of America

CW

10 9 8 7 6 5 4 3 2 1

UGLYDOLLS

Today's the Day!

Adapted by R.R. Busse

LITTLE, BROWN & COMPANY

LB kids

UGLYVILLE

It's another bright, shiny morning in Uglyville. Moxy leaps out of her bed.

Today is THE day!

She runs over to her calendar and writes it down. She's *sure* that today's the day she will be chosen to go to the Big World and meet her human child!

**Moxy is so excited!
She looks at herself in a
mirror and starts singing:**

"Hello, gorgeous.
Let's check out how you look today:
Short and stubby,
Nubby teeth out on full display!
You're pinkish-red,
Got this thing on your head,
And WHOA—
Girl, you couldn't look better!"

Moxy is a reporter. Every day she writes *The Daily Ugly* and delivers her newspapers to all the UglyDolls in Uglyville with her friend Ugly Dog. "Hey, Moxy!" he exclaims. "You're in a good mood!"

"That's because today I'm going to—" Moxy says.

"Get chosen to go to the Big World and be with your child," Ugly Dog interrupts. "You say that every day."

"I know, but today..." Moxy belts out in excitement. "I might be right!"

As Moxy and Ugly Dog make their way through Uglyville, Moxy continues her happy song:

"Shake the sleep off—
And kick into the morning drill.
It's another awesome day
Here in Uglyville!
Grab your shoes,
Time to spread the good news!
Whoa! Things just couldn't be better!
Call it hope or faith, whatever!
I just know in my heart
It's the day I've awaited forever!"

Soon, they pass Wage's bakery. Wage is one of the best—if not *the* best—bakers in all of Uglyville. *"Mornin', Moxy!"* she sings through her window.

"Got something new you'll wanna try:
It's a brownie-cupcake-fudge-berry-ice-cream pie!
Just one bite—who needs kids, am I right?"

Moxy tries the crazy-delicious dessert while Wage tosses some to Babo, who is fixing the outside of the bakery.

Babo is probably the strongest—and the sweetest—UglyDoll around. He's *always* hungry, and he can eat a whole pie in one bite!

Next, Ugly Dog and Moxy see Ox and Lucky Bat.
Ox is the mayor of Uglyville and knows that it's been
a long time since an UglyDoll was chosen to go to the
Big World. He doesn't want Moxy to be disappointed.

Ox hopes Lucky Bat will be able to talk some
sense into her. Lucky Bat is Ox's most trusted
advisor, and he's widely known as the wisest of
all the UglyDolls.

The UglyDolls have a great time together, but Moxy can't stop thinking about meeting her child!

"When someone gets chosen, do you think they get picked up in a giant stretch dune buggy?" she asks.

Ox tries to distract Moxy.

"All this business about the so-called Big World and children...It's just a fairy tale," he explains.

"Everyone says that, but what's the harm in believing?" Moxy asks.

"Never mind that," Ox starts to sing.

"I'll tell you what the day will bring—
First a shindig,
Then a bash, then more partying.
Top it all
With a rave, then a ball."

Suddenly, music fills the air and all the UglyDolls sing and dance together.

Ugly Dog jumps onstage and gets a chance to combine his three passions: rapping, sunglasses, and backup lobsters.

Ox wants to remind Moxy she has everything she needs here, so he gives this song his all!

After his saxophone solo, he points out that Uglyville is the best place to be:

"You know it couldn't be better!"

Moxy gets into the groove after all her friends have joined in:

"And soon, you-know-what is comin'!"
"But until it arrives,
Might as well keep the party hummin'!"

the UglyDolls sing together.

After waiting and hoping all day, Moxy is a little sad. She wasn't picked for the Big World.

What if Ox is right? What if it really is all make-believe?

It can't be! If Moxy isn't going to get picked to meet her child...she'll pick her child herself!

Moxy gathers all her friends and declares, "We're gonna make our dreams come true!" With Lucky Bat, Wage, Ugly Dog, and Babo, she sets off to find the Big World. But what they find instead is a mysterious tunnel.

Inside, the UglyDolls see a giant slide. The only way to see what's at the end of the slide is to *take it*!

At the bottom, they find themselves in front of a place called the Institute of Perfection. They don't know what "perfection" is! They just know about being themselves.

Finding their kids might be harder than Moxy and her friends had thought. But anything is possible with good friends. And who knows, tomorrow might just be...*the day*!

UGLY DOG

#UGLY

STAY UGLY

MOXY

OX

BUFF
Ugly Friends Forever

LUCKY BAT

WAGE

MOXY

BABO